Usborne First Experiences

Going on a plane

Anne Civardi
Illustrated by Stephen Cartwright
Language Consultant: Betty Root

There is a little yellow duck hiding on every page. Can you find it?

The Tripps

This is the Tripp Family. Tim and Rosie are helping Mum and Dad to pack. Tomorrow they are going on holiday.

Off to the airport

The next day, Grandpa drives them to the airport. Lily is staying behind with Granny and Toto, the dog.

At the airport

At the airport, Dad puts the luggage on to a trolley.
"Catch it," he shouts, as one of the bags topples over.

Checking in

"Here are the tickets," says Mum to the hostess at the check-in counter. Another hostess weighs their luggage.

Security check

Before they get on the plane, the Tripps go through a metal detector. Their bags go through an X-ray machine.

On the plane

On the plane, a stewardess shows them to their seats.
Dad puts their bags into a locker above their heads.

Ready for take-off

"Fasten your seat belts. We're about to take off," says the stewardess. "I've strapped Hippo in," says Rosie.

Taking off

The stewardess tells the passengers the safety rules. The pilot starts up the engines of the big plane.

He waits for his turn to take off. Then the plane speeds down the runway and zooms up into the air.

Lunch time

"Here's your lunch," says the stewardess to Mum.
A steward gives Dad a little bottle of wine.

On the flight deck

After lunch, Rosie and Tim go to the flight deck to meet the pilots. "Look at all those knobs," says Tim.

Landing

Before they land, Mum and Rosie go to the toilet. Back in their seats, they listen to music on earphones.

Tim looks out of the window. "We're coming down," he shouts. Soon the plane lands safely on the runway.

Off the plane

At the airport, the Tripps get off the plane down some big steps. "My hat," shouts Mum, as it blows away.

Passport control

They show their passports to an officer. "Look, Dad," says Rosie, "he's putting a big stamp in yours."

Collecting the luggage

They collect their luggage when it comes off the plane.
"Here are my things," Rosie says to a porter.

Outside the airport

Mum gives the porter some money. "Taxi, taxi," shouts
Dad. And off the Tripps go to start their holiday.

First published in 1988. This enlarged edition first published in 1992. Usborne Publishing Ltd, 83-85 Saffron Hill, London EC1N 8RT, England. © Usborne Publishing Ltd, 1992.